Peace, Love and Re

Written by Jenni Smith
Illustrated by Joy Schaber

benefitting embrace compassion

For Julian Peace
and his amazing Family

Julian loves the farm.
He walks the acres in his red shoes.

"Hey there Chickadee," says Julian.

"Cluck-cluck-a-doo-boo-hoo-hoo," Clucks Chickadee, "I'm so fowl fowl blue."

Julian loves the farm.
He walks the acres in his red shoes.

"Hey there Go-Ga-Go-Goat,"
says Julian.

"Nay-oh-nay all the day-oh-day," bleats Goat.
"I've got the sky gray buckling blues."

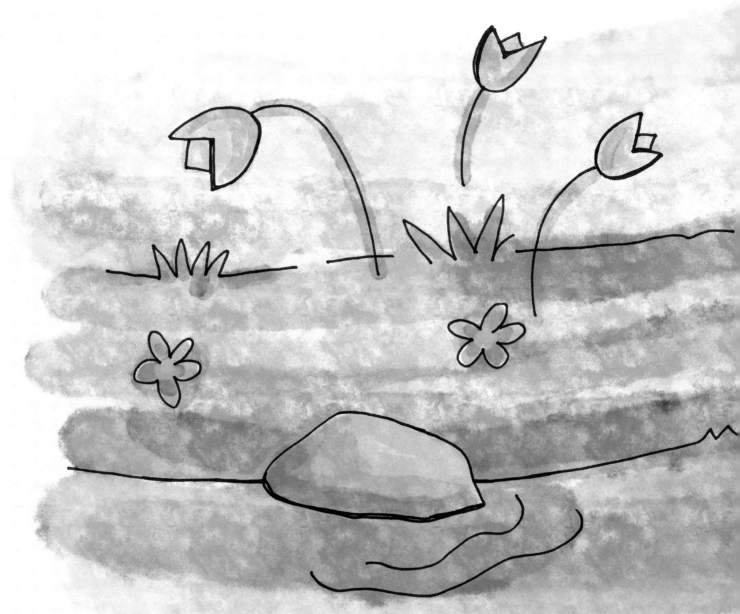

Julian loves the farm.
He walks the acres in his red shoes.

"Peace to you. Don't be blue.
Swim in your red shoes."

Julian gives Lucky Duck a slick
pair of red water shoes.
She splishes, she splashes,
she dives away her blues in
her red shoes.

Julian loves the farm.
He walks the acres in his red shoes.

"Hey there, Sir Harley the Hound"
says Julian.

"Aw-rooh-hoo-roo, Aw-rooh-hoo-roo,"
howls Harley Hound. "I'm so dog gone blue."

"Peace to you. Don't be blue.
Track in your red shoes."

Julian gives Harley
Hound a fast pair of
tracking shoes.

He sniffs, he sprints, he
tracks away his blues in his
red shoes.

Julian loves the farm.
He walks the acres in his red shoes.

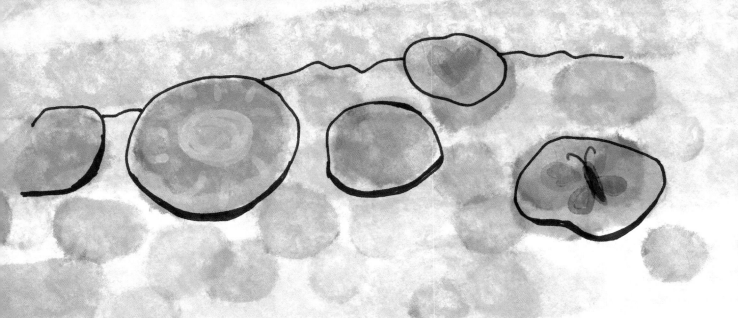

Julian loves the farm.
He walks the acres in his red shoes.

Hey there,
lovely and beautiful reader you.

Could you have the sad, mad, or
sore sore blues?

Peace to you. Don't be blue.
Put on a pair of fancy, splashy shoes and
dance, hop, and skip away your blues.

Psalm 34:14
. . . do good. Search for peace,
and work to maintain it.

God wants us to help each other when
we are mad, sad, or sore. Do you need
to help someone dance, skip, or hop
away their blues? It's up to you to help
them put on their red shoes.

Nagaan lafarra haa buufatu.
(African saying)
May peace prevail on earth.

In loving memory of
Julian Peace

embrace compassion

Find out more about Julian's farm at
embracecompassion.org
and the experiences offered for children with
cancer and their families. Charitable donations
make brighter moments at the farm possible.
Everyone can make someone's life brighter!